PICKER McCLIKKER

By Allen Johnson, Jr.

Illustrations by **Stephen Hanson**

ISBN 1-878561-20-0

Written by Allen Johnson, Jr.
Cover and book illustrations by Stephen Hanson
Book design by Lori Leath-Smith

For Sam and Ben

For Walker
from Picker and...

Alm Johnson
10/5/94

Alright younguns, I know you want to know about my little brother, Picker. You all come on over here by the fire and get comfortable, and I'll tell you the story. That's it, pull down some cushions and set on the floor if you want to.

Well now, did you know Picker's real name was Joe? To understand how it all came about, you got to know about the McClikker family...

We were all growing up during the 1930s when times were hard. Daddy farmed about a hundred acres of cotton on shares which meant that he didn't own the land and had to give back part of the crop in rent.

1

We lived in a little frame house with a tin roof, and we had a big oak shade tree out front that helped to keep the front porch cool in the summer. There was a red dirt farm road that ran near the house with a barbed wire fence alongside that was covered in honeysuckle. In the summer it smelled just wonderful. We lived in the country near Evergreen, Alabama.

There never was much money, but Daddy made enough to buy corn meal and dried black-eyed peas, and we had a cow and chickens, and Mamma grew sweet corn and greens and such, so there was usually enough to eat.

Daddy raised a hog now and then, so sometimes we had ham or bacon. Sometimes there was a bone for our dog whose *name* was "Bone," which was short for bone-lazy. It was a family joke. Mamma'd say, "Johnny, give that bone to Bone," and we always thought it was funny.

There were five of us kids—three boys and two girls. There was me, Johnny McClikker Jr., Rufus, Sally, Amy Lou and Joe, the littlest. I was ten, Rufus seven, Sally six, Amy Lou four and Joe was two and a half. I helped Daddy in the fields after school, and Rufus and Sally did chores, but Amy Lou and Joe were so young they mostly played around the yard.

3

One evening in early summer we had finished supper and were all sitting on the front porch enjoying the cool and smelling the honeysuckle. Daddy was in the swing with his banjo, puffin' on his pipe and strummin' a chord or two.

4

Mamma was in the rocker with Amy Lou in her lap, and the rest of us were playing, when Bone slunk up on the porch. He had gotten into a patch of burrs and was stuck up with em' something awful, from his whiskers to his tail.

5

We all started to laugh, and Bone sat down looking mighty sad. When we stopped, Joe, who just could walk, toddled over to Bone and sat down, kerplop, and said:

"Poor Bone. I gonna fix him."

6

We were all watching, when he reached his hands to Bone and then, it's hard to say what happened, but his hands seemed to move like a blur. Then there was some dog hair drifting around in the air and the neatest pile of burrs you ever saw. Bone was clean as a whistle, waggin' his tail and practically grinning! Joe said, "me fix 'im."

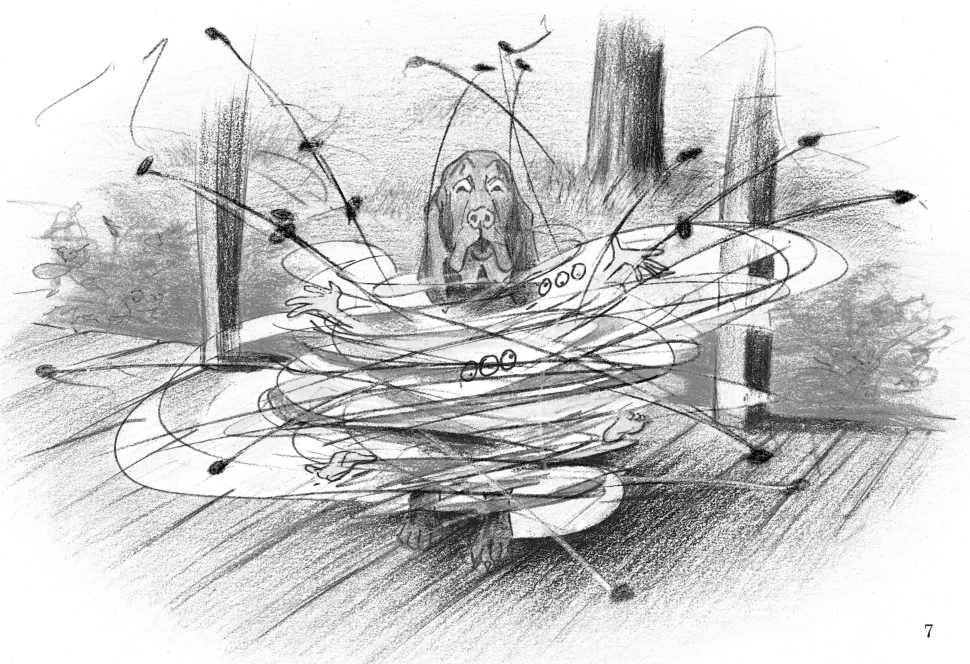

"What in the world!" Daddy said. "Alice, did you see that?"

"I think I did," said Mama, "but I don't believe it! Did baby Joe just pick about a hundred burrs off Bone in

8   about three seconds?"

"I think he *did,* Alice. Fast! That boy's a pickin' fool! I've never seen the like!"

Us kids were impressed too, 'cause Daddy didn't get excited too often, but you know how kids are. By the next day, we had forgotten about it. Mamma hadn't, though.

9

I guess it was three or four months after this that Mamma was out in the garden picking some peas. She got to remembering Joe with the burrs and decided to give him a basket and try him out on peas. He'd been watching her do it, so I guess he knew what to do, 'cause by the time Mamma had walked 20 feet to the porch for another basket and walked back to the pea patch, Joe had picked the whole row clean! Course he couldn't reach the tops of the pea vines, but he sure got every one he could reach. Then Mamma took him up on the porch and showed him how to shell peas. Joe was a quick study! Inside of a minute there were about three quarts of peas

shelled out pretty as you please with the pods all lined up in a nice neat pile. Mamma said: "That boy is a natural born picker!"

Rufus, who had come in from doing his chores, had been watching. He grinned at little Joe, mussed his hair and said, "Picker McClikker!" The name stuck, and Joe was "Picker" from then on.

Well, after awhile, we all got to taking Picker for granted. We knew he had a talent, but we didn't pay too much attention. If Mamma had stuff to be picked out in the garden, Picker would do it before you could blink, but mostly, Picker was a slow, dreamy little boy.

11

He liked to be outside. Sometimes he'd walk across the field out back to Leafy Creek and lie on his stomach looking down in the creek, looking for crawfish. He could grab one out of the water and never get pinched. Sometimes I'd see him out in the yard lying on his back with his head on Bone watching the clouds.

I knew what he was doin' 'cause Daddy had showed us how to see animals in the clouds. Picker was a happy little guy who would sometimes just laugh over a funny thought, but he never talked much. If he could get by with one word, he'd never use two. It wasn't 'til Picker was almost four years old that we really found out what he could do.

It was during the cotton harvest; Daddy and us older kids had come out of the fields to get some lunch. We had about half the crop in, and Daddy was worried. The sky was real black over in the West. It looked like a bad storm coming. Daddy said we should just grab a bite and get back in the field to try to save the rest of the crop. We knew we'd never do it, though. Picker was tugging on Daddy's overalls.

14   "Picker help." Daddy looked down.

"What, son? Oh, thank you son. I know how good you can pick, but you're too young to work in the fields."
"No Daddy. Picker help!"
"O. K., son, *everybody* can help! You come too, Alice. Johnny, run to the barn and get the rest of the bags. Throw 'em in the wagon and hitch up Glory. Bring the wagon out and meet us in the south field!"

15

By the time I got back to the field with the wagon, the lightning was poppin' and the thunder was

16 whangin' way too close for comfort. Glory was skittish, and I had my hands full keeping her from running off.

There seemed to be a little dust storm out there in the field, moving down the rows of cotton. When I got closer, I saw that the dust storm was Picker, arms a-blur. About every five seconds he'd drop a full bag of cotton.

18 Sally and Amy Lou were following him with empty bags. They'd hold one out to Picker, but you couldn't see him grab it. It would just sort of disappear.

The girls had only a few bags left, but Rufus ran over and grabbed a double arm-load out of the wagon.

When he saw that Picker was doing a row every minute, Daddy quit pickin' and jumped in the wagon with me. We came along behind Picker, loading up the wagon with the full bags he'd left between the rows. When we got to the end of the field, I saw Mr. Crocker, who owned the land Daddy farmed, standing by the fence watching. His jaw had fallen open and he was shaking his head like he couldn't believe his eyes.

Well, it took Picker about 15 minutes to clean the rest of that field! Our mule, Glory, was all lathered up from running the wagon to the barn and back, and I had a sore rear end from bouncing on the wagon seat, but we got the crop in!

We got Glory in the barn and ran for the porch. Just then the storm hit. Sheets of rain and hail big as hickory nuts. "Whoee!" Daddy hollered. He swung Picker up on his shoulders and we all started hollerin' and dancing around like a bunch of crazy folks. The rain blew in on the porch and we all got wet, but we were hot and sweaty, and it felt *wonderful*!

A few days later Will Crocker told Amos Burdash about Picker's amazing performance in the cotton field. Amos was the editor of the town newspaper, "The Courant," and he didn't waste a bit of time. He drove his old Ford out to our place to talk to daddy about an idea he had. . .

23

"John" he said, "can this boy of yours pick grapes?"

"Picker can pick *anything,*" Daddy said. "Why do you want to know, Amos?"

Mr. Burdash said, "John, I've got an idea. You probably never heard about it, but there is a big grape picking contest in France next month. . ."

"France!" daddy hollered, "Amos, you must be. . ."

"Listen, John. There's a prize, cash money, five thousand dollars. I think this boy of yours could win it." Daddy sat down in the swing lookin' like he'd been hit between the eyes with a two-by-four.

"Lord, Amos, that's a lot of money! You must be foolin' me. I could never get Picker over to France. I can barely keep shoes on these younguns, much less buy a ticket to France."

"Not one ticket, John, *two*. One for Picker and one for Alice, but the newspaper will pay for the trip. Here is something else, the champion grape picker in France is a 300-pound Gypsy called Big Louis Girard. Look here, I got a picture of him. Think of what a story it would be if Big Louie got beat by a four-year-old from Evergreen, Alabama! It could put Evergreen on the map!"

"Lord!" said Daddy who seemed to be pared down to one word, then Mamma chimed in:

"France, John, just think of it! I've never been further than Montgomery. Oh John, can we go?"   25

I guess it had finally sunk in on Daddy, 'cause he leaned back in the swing with a twinkle in his eye and grinned at Mamma fondly.

26

"Alice, I'm gonna miss you bad, but there ain't no way on God's earth I'd let you miss out on going to France." Good thing there was a strong chain on the swing 'cause Mamma jumped in his lap and gave him such a kiss that us kids got embarrassed.

27

A week after this we were down at the station waving good-bye to Mamma and Picker as the train pulled out.

29

After that we read about them in the newspaper, but we didn't get the whole story 'till Mamma got back
and told us what really happened.

Mamma said it was embarrassing when they got to Bordeaux, France, and met Big Louis. Instead of shaking hands with Picker, Big Louis fell on the ground holding his sides, laughing 'til tears poured down his face, stopping only long enough to point at Picker in amazement only to start laughing all over again. It made

Picker mad which is hard to do. Picker said to Mamma:

"Mr. Big Louis not gonna laugh so hard tomorrow!", which was the longest sentence anybody had heard out of Picker.

Well the next day they were out in the vineyard early. Each picker in the contest had his own row of grapes in a big square field. All the rows were the same length. Whoever got to the end first was gonna be the champion. Big Louis had heard that Picker had never picked grapes before and started to laugh all over again.

Then he told the judges to take Picker over in another field and let him practice so he wouldn't be so embarrassed in the contest. Picker stood there with his arms folded over his chest and said: "No thank you Mr. Judge. Picker don't need practice." True! Very true, as it turned out.

The judge fired a gun to start the contest, and Big Louis was just finishing off his fourth vine when
another gun went off at the end of the field where Picker had finished. Big Louis looked stunned.

"Mon Dieu!" he said, "C'est impossible!" (which means something like, "Lord have mercy! That's impossible!")

It was quite a shock for Big Louis, but he turned out to have a heart as big as the rest of him, 'cause when Picker got the prize, Big Louis gave a very warm speech. He said it was an honor to be beaten by "Monsieur Piquer," the greatest "piquer" that the world would ever know. ("Piquer" was as close as the French could come to "Picker." It sounded something like "Peecur"!)

Picker loved France, but he said he didn't like to be called no "Peecur"! Anyway, there was a victory parade, and Big Louis carried Picker all around Bordeaux on his shoulder while folks cheered and threw flowers. Two weeks later the world's champion grape picker came home to Evergreen, Alabama.

It did put Evergreen on the map, too. All the big newspapers picked up the story of the four-year-old champion grape picker. Picker was famous, but he didn't seem to care. He just went right back to being a normal little boy, only more dreamy and peaceful than most. Daddy wanted to put the prize money in the bank for Picker to have for college, but Picker said he wanted us to own our piece of land and our little house so Daddy

used the money for that, but he put the house and land in Picker's name. There was enough left over for Daddy to buy a tractor, so he could farm a little easier, and our hard-working mule, Glory, could retire. Then Picker went downtown with Mamma and bought us all something.

Mamma got some pretty new dresses, and we all got new clothes and shoes, but we each got something special, too. Amy Lou got a beautiful doll; Sally, who was a tomboy, got a baseball glove and a ball; and me and Rufus got Red Rider BB guns. Boy was that exciting! Then Daddy asked Picker what *he* wanted.

42

"Picker want a pretty banjo like Daddy play," he said.
"Why, shore!" said Daddy. "No reason why a champion picker can't pick a banjo!"

Well, you might guess what happened when Picker got a hold of that banjo, but that's another story; one I aim to tell you next time. Right now, let's all get us a cool glass of milk and a cookie before bed. If you all come back tomorrow, I promise to tell you 'bout how Picker and his banjo made things a whole lot better for all us McClikkers.

'Night, younguns. Sleep tight!